My Bindi

For my mother, Raji, who wears a bindi everyday,
even when she sleeps. — G.V.

For Inji, who is always unabashedly,
unapologetically herself. — A.S.

Library of Congress Cataloging-in-Publication Data available

ISBN 978-1-338-59881-0

10 9 8 7 6 5 4 3 2 1   22 23 24 25 26

Printed in China 62
First edition, Feburary 2022
Book design by Rae Crawford

The text type was set in Rotis Semi Sans Std.
The display type was hand drawn by Rae Crawford.

The illustrations were created with pencil on paper, along with digital coloring.

My Bindi

Written by **Gita Varadarajan**

Illustrated by **Archana Sreenivasan**

Orchard Books
New York
An Imprint of Scholastic Inc.

My mother, my amma, places a big red dot on her forehead.
She wears a bindi every day . . .
even when she sleeps.

Amma says I should wear the bindi too,
but I'm scared —
of Sam snickering at me,
of Sally taking it off my forehead,
of Sania saying, "Weirdo,"
even though Sania is Indian too.

"But it's our culture," Amma says.
"There's nothing to be ashamed of,"
my father reminds me.
"You'll look so beautiful with a bindi on!"

"But, Amma, why do you wear a bindi?" I ask.
Amma thinks a minute.
In her eyes I see a candle flame light up.
Then she touches her bindi and says,
"We are Hindus, and that's what Hindu girls do.
It's our third eye, right between the other two.
It looks inside you and protects you."

I wonder deep down what she means.
"You'll feel it," she says, "when you wear it."

That night I toss and turn in bed.
And dream of the big red dot on Amma's forehead.

As I get dressed for school the next morning,
Amma walks in with a box in her hand.
A smile flickers across her face.
Then she says, "Divya, my dear,
the time has come. Choose one."

I swallow hard and look inside
Amma's beautiful bindi box.
I see a galaxy of bindis —
like a million stars in the sky.

Some are like raindrops that dazzle in the morning light.
Some are like half-moons, brilliant and bright.
Some swirl like tops whirling in loops.
Some shine like lone stars in a dark sky.
I search through them all, each one so beautiful in its own way.

Then I see it!
The perfect one,
a blazing sun,
a sparkly, round orange one,
with a shiny stone in the middle.

"Here," I say nervously, handing it to Amma.
Her bangles clang as she lifts my chin —
and looks at the space between my brows.
Then she gently presses the bindi to my forehead.

My forehead feels heavy,
and my heart feels full.
It's beating so hard, it might explode.

"Now take a look," Amma says.

There in the mirror,
I see a shining star.
My mother's joy.
My father's pride.
And then I see something else.
She's different from all the rest,
not quite like anyone else,
with a glimmering dot
on her forehead.
I see me.

Am I scared
or am I proud?
I feel all mixed up
in my head.

I walk into school, like I always do,
but I'm nervous. Because today is different in one big way.

"What's that?" Sam asks curiously,
pointing at my forehead.

"That looks cool!" Sally says as she tries to get a closer look.
Sania's eyes go wide with surprise . . .
"It's a bindi," she says loudly.
Suddenly everyone wants to see!

"What's all the commotion?"
Mrs. Gonzalez asks, clapping her hands.

"Look at Divya's forehead!"

Mrs. Gonzalez squints.

My heart skips a beat.

I wonder what she will say.

Then I hear a voice, soft like gently lapping waves.
"Divya," says Mrs. Gonzalez,
"would you like to come up and tell the class
about what you are wearing?"

I nod and walk up slowly to the front of the class.
My lips quiver, my shoulders scrunch up,
and my stomach tightens.

I am different from all the rest,
not quite like anyone else,
with a glimmering dot on my forehead.

Thoughts come and
go like floating clouds.
And then . . .

I see something else.
A shining star.
My mother's joy.
My father's pride.
I see ME.

I run my hand around my bindi.
And suddenly
I can feel it.
Just like Amma said.

I take a deep breath and
straighten my shoulders.
Be brave, I pray, looking up
at the bindi on my forehead,
and slowly the words come cascading
like a soft waterfall.

"This is my bindi," I say.
"It's more than just a dot —
It's my third eye, right between the other two.
It can see inside me and protect me."

I touch my bindi and I know
I am not scared anymore.

Now I wear a new bindi every day to school.
Some are like raindrops that dazzle
in the morning light.
Some are like half-moons, brilliant and bright.
Some swirl like tops whirling in loops.
Some shine like lone stars in a dark sky.

It's my inner eye,
my guardian,
my bindi . . .

It makes me feel like ME
and I can't imagine my face without it.

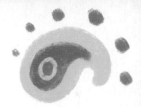

AUTHOR'S NOTE

The bindi is worn by many Hindu girls and women in India and derives from the Sanskrit word "bindu," which means drop. It is traditionally worn as a red dot between the eyebrows, a spot that is considered to be the nerve point in the human body that releases energy. In ancient Hindu tradition, it signifies the third inner eye. The two physical eyes are for seeing the outside world, while the third focuses on the inside. Red in Hindu culture is also a symbol of prosperity, hence the red dot is considered an auspicious sign.

Today, not everyone strictly follows the tradition of wearing a bindi. For some, it has become a fashion accessory, but for many it remains a powerful symbol, and a tradition that families continue to pass along to younger generations. The red dot has been replaced by all kinds of colors and shapes. It can be an oval or a triangle, and can be encrusted with glittering stones or studded with beads.

I remember the face of a little girl I met while on a school visit in Edison, New Jersey. She was sitting in the front row during the assembly, a wide smile on her face and a bright, shiny bindi on her forehead. The image stayed with me for a long time. It became the inspiration for this story.

I find that some youngsters of Indian ethnicity in America are reticent to reveal their traditions. As they live up to the model minority narrative, the idea of assimilating and fitting in is conveyed to them at a very young age. I wrote this story to give every little Hindu girl the courage to embrace her culture and traditions, just like that little girl did in Edison with her wide smile and her bright, shiny bindi.

—Gita Varadarajan

ILLUSTRATOR'S NOTE

My sister and I grew up as Hindu kids who went to a convent school run by Christian missionaries, as did many others in the 70s and 80s in Bangalore. Our classmates were also largely Hindus, with a few children from other faiths. And yet, when our father urged us to wear a bindi, we almost always refused because we thought it was "uncool." Even though we were very much in India, we still resisted bindis, pattu paavaadais (a traditional South Indian silk skirt and blouse), and many other traditional Indian clothes. We wanted to wear jeans and T-shirts, and short skirts and pointy shoes with heels that click-clacked on the floor when we walked. It was many years later, in my mid-to-late twenties, that I began to have appreciation for things traditionally Indian. As the years go by, and as I get more comfortable in my own skin, this journey of reconnecting with my roots continues. So the transformation that Divya goes through in this book is an ongoing process for me, and one that will go on for many years more, peeling back layer upon layer of everything that makes me, me!

—Archana Sreenivasan